The Day Uncle S[am Lost Hi]s Yankee Doodle Dandy

The Day Uncle Sam Lost His Yankee
Doodle Dandy

Written by   : Brooke Mahaffey

Illustrated by : Sumaiyya Mansoor

The Day Uncle Sam Lost His Yankee Doodle Dandy

The Little Dandelion Press
www.thelittledandelionpress.com

Written by **Brooke Mahaffey**
Illustrated by **Sumaiyya Mansoor**

ISBN: 978-1-7373194-0-5 (paperback)
ISBN: 978-1-7373194-1-2(hardback)

Library Of Congress Control Number : 2021910890

Printed in the United States of America

First Edition: 2021

This book is dedicated to my husband, Jake;
My rock, my cheerleader, my everything.
Thank you for your constant support,
encouragement, and unconditional love.

One summer morning, Uncle Sam woke up bright and early. "What a beautiful day," he told his dog with great excitement. "This is going to be an amazing 4th of July!" Independence Day was Uncle Sam's favorite day of the year! It was the birthday of the nation he LOVED... the U.S. of A.!

He and his dog, Yankee Doodle Dandy, were the most patriotic duo in town and were set to lead the annual 4th of July parade!

Uncle Sam reached down to pat Yankee Doodle Dandy's head, but the pup was not there! "YANKEE!" He called out! "YANKEE DOODLE DANDY!!!"

He had to find his dog if they were to lead the parade that afternoon. It simply would not do without good ol' Yankee Doodle Dandy!

He jumped out of bed and called his nephew, Johnny Appleseed, for help.

Ring, Ring!

"Hello?" Johnny answered.

"Wake up, Johnny! Yankee Doodle Dandy is MISSING!"

Johnny quickly rushed over to help.
"Where should we look first?"

8

"If I were Yankee Doodle Dandy, where might I be? He loves the home of the brave and the land of the free!"

"Home of the brave... That's it! Of course! Where else but the White House? Follow me!"

"It's been home to every President, excep for George Washington," explained Uncl Sam. "The President lives in an apartmer at the top and works from the Oval Office.

They searched high; they searched low.
They searched fast; they searched slow.
They looked left; they looked right.
Yankee Doodle Dandy wasn't anywhere in sight.

11

"No sign of him here," said Johnny. "Where should we look next?"

"If I were Yankee Doodle Dandy, where might I be?

He loves the home of the brave and the land of the free!"

"Let's try the Washington Monument!" Uncle Sam suggested.

Yankee Doodle Dandy was always impressed that it stands 555 feet tall! It's made entirely of stone and was built for our first president, George Washington!"

They searched high; they searched low.
They searched fast; they searched slow.
They looked left; they looked right.
Yankee Doodle Dandy wasn't anywhere in sight.

"I'm sorry he's not here!" Johnny said. "I'm not quite sure where to look for him next."

"If I were Yankee Doodle Dandy, where might I be? He loves the home of the brave and the land of the free!"

16

"Land of the free…" Thought Johnny. "And who led more to freedom than our 16th President, Abraham Lincoln? "To the Lincoln Memorial, let's go!"

17

"Great thinking, Johnny!" replied Uncle Sam. "He led the country during the American Civil War, and he delivered the famous Gettysburg Address.

They searched high; they searched low.
They searched fast; they searched slow.
They looked left; they looked right.
Yankee Doodle Dandy wasn't anywhere in sight.

"Another bust!" Johnny sighed. "He's not here, but we won't give up!"
"If I were Yankee Doodle Dandy, where might I be?
He loves the home of the brave and the land of the free!"

"Let's check the Capitol Building," exclaimed Uncle Sam, "Where the US Congress makes new laws. Run to Capitol Hill!"

"There are two chambers on either side of the large dome: The Senate meets in the North Wing and the House of Representatives in the South Wing."

They searched high; they searched low.
They searched fast; they searched slow.
They looked left; they looked right.
Yankee Doodle Dandy wasn't anywhere in sight.

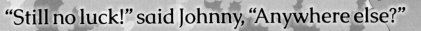

"Still no luck!" said Johnny, "Anywhere else?"

"I have one more patriotic idea up my sleeve. The ultimate symbol of American freedom, Johnny and a gift from France. Can you guess?"

"Of course, Uncle Sam, Yankee Doddle Dandy is in New York! He's at the Statue of Liberty on Ellis Island!"

Uncle Sam and Johnny hopped on a bus to New York City. When they arrived, they whizzed past Central Park and Times Square and headed straight to the Statue of Liberty.

They searched high; they searched low.

They searched fast; they searched slow.

They looked left; they looked right.

And there sat Yankee Doodle Dandy, right there, in the sunlight!

"There you are, at last!" They rejoiced, running to the pup.
"We looked all over for you, silly boy," Uncle Sam cried.

Yankee Doodle licked Uncle Sam and barked, "WOOF! WOOF!!" "You're right, boy! The parade! Let's go; we have just enough time!"

They hopped on the bus and headed back home. They arrived just in time to help kick off the parade.

The whole town lined the streets, with their hands on their hearts, as th
marching band played the Star-Spangled Banner among a sea o
proudly-waved flags.

When the anthem was over, Uncle Sam blew his whistle. Then, they all began marching down the street.

Uncle Sam felt so proud to be a part of America's birthday party!

It was the best 4th of July ever!

Meet the Author

Brooke Mahaffey is a military spouse, mother of three, and an elementary school educator. As an avid reader herself, Brooke enjoys fostering a love of reading in her own children, as well as her students. Brooke's patriotism for her country and her love for celebrating Independence Day inspired her to write this book. In her free time, she enjoys reading, hiking, and traveling with her family.

Brooke is also the author of the book I'm A Dandelion: A PCS Story For Military Children.

If you enjoyed this book, please consider leaving a book review on Amazon. It will help new readers discover similar books and future books by this author.

Made in United States
North Haven, CT
30 May 2023

37157562R00020